INTO THE JUNGLE

Halt, adventurer, and read these words before you proceed!

You are about to embark on a journey. To where, only you could possibly say. It is not a journey like any you have been on before, where you start at page one and continue on a straight course until you reach the end. Instead, you will be presented with many choices along the way. Each time you are faced with one such choice, make your decision from the options given and then follow the directions to continue your adventure. Once your quest has come to an end, either favorably or, as I'm afraid in some instances it is foretold to, gruesomely, return to the beginning or the last choice and try again.

This is not a journey for those who prefer to sit back and let others make the tricky decisions. This is a journey for a leader, a true hero. One who is not afraid to converse with giants, explore the dark and dangerous jungle, or face the undead. If this doesn't sound like you, turn back now and forget you ever came this way. But if this whiff of adventure has whet your appetite, then forward with you, my friend. And good luck!

CANDLEWICK
ENTERTAINMENT

DUNGEONS & DRAGONS

ENDLESS QUEST®

INTO THE JUNGLE

MATT FORBECK

After several stomach-churning weeks at sea aboard a sloop known as the *Brazen Pegasus*, you finally arrive at Port Nyanzaru on the northern shore of the distant continent of Chult. The voyage from Baldur's Gate made for the longest week of your life. Despite the assurances of Captain Ortimay — a wily gnome with a shady past — you never got your sea legs and spent the entire time pitching back and forth across the ship's deck. Dwarves, in your opinion, were never meant to travel by sea, and you had never expected life as a cleric to ever put you upon the water. Is there not enough work to be done on your own shores after all?

You spent most of the trip praying to Clangeddin Silverbeard, the dwarf god of honorable battle to whom you've dedicated your life, hoping that he might be able to deliver you from your seasickness, but that never happened. You were built for the solid stone floors of your ancestral home, Mithral Hall, and wonder now how wise you were to leave it.

The rest of the time you spent cursing the Harpers, the semisecret religious organization you work for, trying to do some good in this dangerous world. It was at their command that you set out for Chult. If not for them, you would never have set foot on a boat or found yourself so far from the comforts of home.

But now here you are, and you have a mission: to find Artus Cimber and the Ring of Winter. Cimber is a legendary member of the Harpers, a man who never ages and has done a world of good. He's gone missing, though, along with his ring, a powerful artifact that — if it fell into the wrong hands — could be used to plunge the world into an eternal winter.

You cannot let this happen.

You stagger down the gangplank from the *Brazen Pegasus* and fall to your knees on the first patch of solid land you can find. You kiss it unashamedly and then offer up prayers of gratitude to Clangeddin for delivering you there alive, if not in absolute comfort.

"Hail and well met, good fellow!" a bushy-bearded man says as he helps you to your feet. "My name is Volothamp Geddarm, but you can call me Volo. All my friends do."

"Do I know you?" you ask, instantly suspicious.

"Of course not," he says with a wide and easy smile. "But I can recognize a fellow intrepid traveler at a giant's pace. I write guidebooks for a living, and my publisher — Tym Waterdeep Limited — sent me here on a tour to help promote my latest tome, *Volo's Guide to Monsters*. Hopefully a good, sensible soul like yourself would never need a copy, though." He gives you a dubious look.

"I'm here on business," you inform the man. "What I really need is someone to guide me."

"Good call!" Volo gives you a jolly slap on the back. "You're almost in the right place. You can find all sorts of them plying their trade here on the docks, but if you head just a little farther into town, I can introduce you to a trusted pair I know. Qawasha is a local druid who works closely with a vegepygmy named Kupalué."

You size the man up. He seems harmless enough, but is he trustworthy? He senses your hesitation and shrugs.

"Feel free to hire someone else, of course, or leg it out there into the jungle on your own. Chult is an amazing land of adventure, and it awaits!"

Find your own guides. Turn to page 6...
Head into the jungle on your own. Turn to page 9...
Hire Qawasha and Kupalué. Turn to page 17...

All right," you say to Faroul as you hand him the rest of your cash. "Crimson Teeth it is. In for a copper, in for a gold, right?"

The man flashes a contagious smile at you. "You're a wise and faithful dwarf, my friend," he says.

He dumps your cash into a purse with everything you've already paid him and then dashes off to place your bets on the gigantic allosaurus.

When the race starts, you're ready to burst with excitement. The dinosaurs scrape and claw at the starting line as if they can barely be contained.

"This is the unchained race," Gondolo explains. "The first two are far more civilized. The dinosaurs are smaller and muzzled to prevent disasters. This challenge, though, is for the greatest, most dangerous racers around, and things can get truly bloody!"

Faroul rejoins you just as the race begins, a huge grin on his face. "We're going to be filthy rich!"

You offer up prayers to Clangeddin that he sees Crimson Teeth through to victory, and then, with a loud bang, the race begins. The dinosaurs take off, rampaging through the streets, and, sure enough, Crimson Teeth is in the lead. Just as he's about to cross the finish line, though, Little Arms comes from behind and tramples him into the ground!

With Crimson Teeth down, you realize you've just lost all your money—and so have your guides. You turn to take out your anger on them at having destroyed your plans, but they're already running away! You take off in pursuit, but with your shorter, dwarven legs there is little hope of you catching them.

"Easy come, easy go!" Faroul shouts as he and Gondolo lose you in the still-cheering crowd.

You never find them, and once you calm down, you realize that someone else is going to have to search for Artus—while you get a job to pay back the Harpers.

THE END

"Thanks for your help," you tell Volo, "but I think I'll find guides of my own." You gather your meager belongings into your pack and head into town. You don't get too far before you are approached by two fellows—a handsome man with dusky skin, and a tubby, pale halfling.

"You seem to be looking for something," the man says with an easy smile. "We're just the people to help you find it. My name is Faroul, and this is my stalwart companion, Gondolo. We're the greatest guides on the entire island. No one knows the jungles of Chult better than we do!"

For some reason, they strike you as experienced people. Perhaps it's because of the triceratops that Gondolo is leading around behind him on a leash. Although you've heard of such creatures, you've never seen such a gigantic lizard in your life. The idea of using an armored, three-horned monstrosity like that as a pack animal thrills you.

You quickly negotiate a fee with Faroul and Gondolo for their services and pay them what seems like an enormous amount up front. Thank Clangeddin the money's coming out of the Harpers' pocket and not your own.

As Faroul stuffs your payment into his purse, he leans in and speaks to you in a confidential tone.

"We could head straight off into the wild, of course, but I can see that you're a sophisticated dwarf.

What would you say to attending the dinosaur races first?"

"They are a sight not to be missed," Gondolo says with a firm nod. "You have nothing of the kind back on the Sword Coast, I'm certain. Plus, we have a hot tip on a sure thing in the third race. Now that we're well funded, it would be a shame to miss out on that."

Head into the jungle. Turn to page 12 . . .
Off to the races! Turn to page 14 . . .

You decide you can't afford to trust any guides, not when you're on such an important mission. There'd be no knowing whether their intentions were pure. And even if the guides were trustworthy, once they knew what you were hunting for, they could easily be swayed by the power offered by the ring. Instead, you buy the best equipment you can find, including an ankylosaurus for a pack animal, and you strike out into the jungle on your own. How hard can navigating the jungle be, anyway?

You follow the western bank of the River Soshenstar deep into the densest vegetation you've ever seen. The canopy of leaves becomes so thick that it blots out the sunlight, casting the jungle floor in deep shadows. It's peaceful here. Almost unbearably quiet, in fact.

As you listen hard for any sign of life, you smell something worse than a rotting swamp. Then you hear a gigantic beast crashing through the jungle as if the trees between it and you were nothing more than straw, and the ground begins to shake.

You look up, and you see it: a gigantic dinosaur walking on its hind feet and growling at the world through yard-long teeth. It's a Tyrannosaurus rex.

You utter a quick prayer to Clangeddin, and with the power he grants you, fire bursts from your hands and runs up your arms. While it can burn your foes, your god protects you from its fiery might. You stick your arms out and wave them in front of you. It may not be the most effective attack, but it's a technique you've used many times before.

This monster doesn't flinch, though, and after a moment, you see why. Its bones are showing through its shredded flesh: a number of ribs, part of its jaw, a whole skeletal arm. Yet it's staggering along just fine. On closer inspection, it is suddenly obvious just how much danger you have found yourself in on this, the first day of your adventure. Stomping its way toward you is a zombie Tyrannosaurus rex!

You spin around and run, leaving your ankylosaurus behind. The creature makes a horrible sound as the gigantic zombie dinosaur tears it to pieces, then everything becomes quiet again. You don't know which is worse.

You run through the jungle in a dead panic until you come to a clearing. It's no time to rest, though. Looking around, you realize you've stumbled into a goblin village, and the little creatures have you surrounded!

While the goblins poke at you with spears, you notice a massive tree bent over the center of the village. Ropes lead off it in numerous places, securing it in its rather peculiar position. You wonder why, until you hear a horrible roar at the edge of the clearing.

The goblins turn and flee, and the tyrannosaurus comes straight at you. With few other options left, you kneel in the dirt and pray to Clangeddin with all your might. "Please deliver me from this creature!" you beg.

The goblins are hacking away at something with axes, and you try hard not to let their labor or the monstrous tyrannosaurus distract you from your prayer. But then the ground beneath you begins to shake, and you can hold your concentration no more. What is this new danger?

Opening your eyes, you study the ground beneath you. A stringy material covers the surface. Puzzled, you adjust your gaze to take it all in and realize that the entire village was built on a gigantic net, which is attached to the tree. The goblins are chopping at the ropes that hold the tree down, and your eyes widen in frightened understanding as the last rope snaps. As the giant tree pings back into its upright position, the net is flung into the air, taking you and every one of the huts in the village with it and depositing it all more than half a mile away.

You get away from the dinosaur, but you can't escape the landing. The village survives, but you do not.

THE END

Y ou insist on being professional and leaving Port Nyanzaru right away.

"Into the jungle it is!" Faroul says, doing his best to mask his disappointment.

They strap your pack on top of their triceratops, which is named Zongo, and set out.

It's hard going, much harder than you would have expected. Gondolo rides atop Zongo while Faroul directs them from behind. You bring up the rear, doing your best not to step in the messes Zongo leaves in his wake.

The sun sets fast in the jungle, and you ask your guides to set up camp for the night.

"Right!" Faroul looks to Gondolo. "Did you remember to pack our camping gear?"

"I thought you had packed it all," the halfling says with a shrug.

"I'm so sorry." Faroul blushes as he apologizes. "We can head back in the morning—we'll never get to town before the darkness takes us tonight."

Fortunately you have your personal gear with you. It should be enough for tonight, even if it means having a cold dinner and breakfast—and that you'll have to share with Faroul and Gondolo.

Turn to page 15 . . .

You say a quick but heartfelt prayer to Clangeddin for guidance on how to bet, and you get a strong feeling that you should go with your gut.

"I like the look of Little Arms," you tell Faroul.

He gives you a friendly you'll-regret-this shrug but agrees to abide by your wishes. He runs off to place your bet—and to put all of his and Gondolo's money down on Crimson Teeth.

The entire town seems to have turned out to cheer the dinosaurs, and you can't help but be caught up in the fever. With a loud bang to start the race, the dinosaurs sprint away from the starting line and are off!

Crimson Teeth takes an early lead, but he gets hung up just before he finishes the first lap. Little Arms pounces on him and takes him down, then races past all the other contestants to win!

When you collect on your bet, you gasp at your winnings. You've never seen so much money at once. You take this as a sign from Clangeddin and decide to use the cash not to find Artus Cimber for the Harpers, but to start a chapel for your generous god instead. You're sure the Harpers will understand.

THE END

How lucky that you arrived in town on race day," Faroul says. "This happens only once a week!"

"Even luckier that you found us," Gondolo says in a sly whisper. "If you have any more money, we'd be happy to put it down on Crimson Teeth for you."

You watch the jockeys parade the brightly painted dinosaurs down the street, bringing them to the starting line, and you can hardly believe your eyes. Their roars send chills down your spine even as the crowds send up cheers.

"He's the allosaurus over there," Gondolo says, pointing to a massive creature with foot-long teeth.

"What about that one?" you ask, pointing at an even taller beast.

"Ah," Faroul says with a smile. "The tyrannosaurus is a majestic beast, to be sure, but Little Arms there won't be in the winner's circle today!"

When Little Arms roars, though, you're not so sure you can believe that.

Bet on Crimson Teeth. Turn to page 4...
Put your money on Little Arms. Turn to page 13...

You grumble about it, but you bed down under the jungle's thick canopy. Tomorrow, once you get back to town, you plan to find yourself better guides.

As you're trying to sleep, you hear a horrible hooting sound out of the darkness beyond the campfire, and you leap to your feet, your sacred hammer in your hand.

"Gods," Faroul says, trembling. "That's the call of the mighty girallon."

"The what?"

"Massive four-armed, white-furred gorillas that have developed a distinct taste for meat."

The hooting grows louder, and now you can hear it coming from at least three directions at once.

"What do we do?" Gondolo asks, whimpering.

You see three sets of eyes glittering back at you from the darkness.

"Run," you tell Faroul and Gondolo as you ready your hammer for what will be your final battle. "Run!"

You pray to Clangeddin that this will, at least, be a quick death.

THE END

At your request, Volo takes you to the guides he mentioned and introduces you.

"This is Qawasha," he says, "the best guide in all of Chult. He and his stalwart companion Kupalué can take care of you from here."

With that he turns and quickly disappears into the crowd, leaving you with your new guides.

You regard them cautiously. Qawasha is a local man, tall and dark with an easy smile. Kupalué is like nothing you've ever seen: the size and shape of a halfling but seemingly made entirely of green mold. He doesn't say a word, but he and Qawasha communicate using hand signals.

"Happy to help any who come to our land, especially a cleric like yourself," Qawasha says, recognizing the amulets around your neck as he offers you his hand in greeting. "The undead have become a plague upon Chult, and anything you can do to help rid us of them will be appreciated."

You take his hand and give it a firm but quick shake.

"That's not my purpose here, but I'm always eager to help drive such horrors from the world," you respond.

"Excellent," Qawasha says with a wide smile. Kupalué pounds the end of his spear on the ground in agreement, causing little puffs of spores to rise from his skin.

Qawasha notices the uneasy glance you give his friend and broadens his smile in what you assume is meant to be reassurance.

"Don't worry," he says. "The mold that animates vegepygmies like my friendly weed here isn't contagious."

Despite your unease, you hire the pair, and the three of you immediately set out for Fort Beluarian, a short journey to the north.

"It's run by these Flaming Fist mercenaries," Qawasha explains. "They claim control over the territory you want to explore, and all adventurers need to purchase a charter from them to have permission to wander about Chult."

"Or?"

"They throw you in chains. If it's not more convenient to kill you on the spot."

Kupalué draws a thin finger across his throat.

You gape at your guides. "That sounds like extortion."

"Then your ears are on right," Qawasha says. "Welcome to Chult!"

"But I'm not here to loot tombs," you say. "I'm just looking for one person."

Qawasha shrugs. "We can try to explain that to the Flaming Fists if they find us. They might even listen for a bit before they attack."

Resigned to the unfairness of the situation, you follow Qawasha's guidance and make your way to Fort Beluarian. There you find Commander Liara Portyr, who agrees to sell you a charter at a hefty price—almost every bit of money you have left. You swallow your indignation and pay the fee.

"That's just an advance for us," Liara tells you. "It pays for the first part of our half of all the treasure you haul out of the jungle."

You almost choke at the way she's trying to rob you

and decide not to tell her there's no way she can have half of the only treasure you care about: the Ring of Winter.

The next day, well-rested and with charter in hand, you take off into the jungle to look for Artus Cimber. Qawasha lays out your options for you.

"There are two ways to head out from here. We can either march toward Camp Righteous or toward Kir Sabal."

You give him a blank look, and he explains your options further.

"Camp Righteous is run by the Order of the Gauntlet, a group of templars who see it as their holy mission to rid the world of the scourge of the undead. They're good people, if perhaps a bit arrogant. Their camp is off to the southwest,

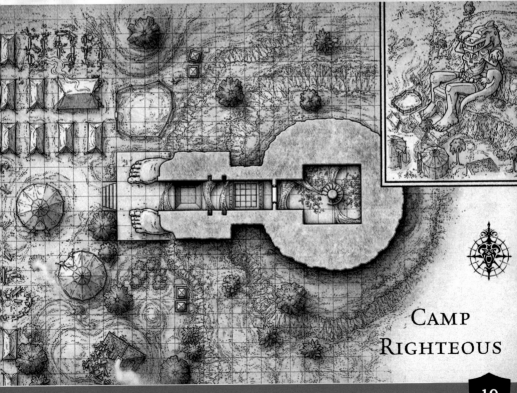

CAMP
RIGHTEOUS

and there's no one who knows the western part of the island better than they do."

"And Kir Sabal?" you ask.

"Kir Sabal, to the southeast, is an ancient monastery run by a tribe of aarakocra, a kind of bird-people with heads like eagles. Because they can fly, they can see all over. No one knows the eastern part of the island better than they do."

Kupalué stares straight at you with eager, unblinking eyes as Qawasha says to you, "It's your call, boss. Which way do you want to go?"

You mull your options carefully, eager to complete your mission as quickly and cleanly as possible so you can get back home.

Head for Camp Righteous. Turn to page 26...
Head for Kir Sabal. Turn to page 28...

Kupalué stabs a finger toward a patch of sky, and when you look up, you spy a flock of pterafolk winging their way toward you. They have long pointed heads, and their leathery wings stretch wide to catch the air beneath them. They're moving your way fast, and you feel your hand itching for your war hammer's grip.

Kupalué readies his spear to hurl at the creatures, but Qawasha gestures at him to lower it. Then he curses your luck and then turns to you for advice.

"We can try to fight them if you like," Qawasha says. "Perhaps your dwarf battle god will give us the edge we'd need. Were Kupalué and I here alone, though, we would never attempt it. It would be simpler to lose ourselves in the jungle, either to the east or the beneath the canopies where such flyers are loath to follow. But this is your mission, so we will follow your lead. What will it be?"

Head east into the jungle. Turn to page 31 . . .
Fight the pterafolk! Turn to page 33 . . .
Head south into the jungle. Turn to page 36 . . .

Your guides start creeping forward into the camp. Not wanting to be left alone in a zombie-infested jungle, you follow close behind.

The camp looks more like a shrine to a long-forgotten god. There are all sorts of tents and pens and such—the kind you'd find in any military camp—but they stand empty in front of a large statue set into the face of a nearby cliff. It's eighty feet tall and resembles a man carrying a crocodile on his back.

"What is that?" you ask, mystified.

"The House of the Crocodile," Qawasha says. "It's a shrine to a deal that people made with crocodiles in ancient times that causes them to be enemies to this day. You can get into it through that archway beneath the man's feet, but everyone who's ever tried has paid the ultimate price."

You peer at it curiously. Were you here to plunder tombs and shrines, you might give the House of the Crocodile a try, but you suspect that Artus Cimber wouldn't have entered such a place.

As you wander through the rest of the camp, Kupalué stamps his spear on the ground and signals for a halt.

"What is it?" Qawasha asks.

The vegepygmy points toward the edge of the forest, and you instantly see what he's spotted. A half dozen or so goblins staring back at you from the shadows!

You begin stalking toward the creatures, unwilling to wait for them to stab you in the back. As you do, a pair of them stand up and blast away on horns, the peals of which echo throughout the jungle. A moment later, you hear the rattling of bones and the sound of dead groans emerging from the jungle to your left. Zombies and skeletons!

Fight them! Turn to page 35 . . .
Run! Turn to page 40 . . .

While you hate to delay your search for Artus Cimber, you can't turn away from so many soldiers in such dire need. You agree to transport them back upriver on the condition that Breakbone helps you find Cimber upon your return. He gives you a weak smile of relief, an emotion you think he might not have felt for weeks.

You and your guides load up a boat with sick soldiers and set out for Port Nyanzaru.

"Why didn't we use a boat to come upriver?" you ask Qawasha.

He shrugs. "Boats are expensive, and they are much easier to ride downriver than to paddle upriver. Plus the waters have a habit of hiding the kind of dangers you just don't find on dry land."

You're not much good in a boat, but you set to helping the ill soldiers as best you can. They seem grateful for all that you do.

That evening, as the sun sets, you hear a loud noise that vibrates the entire boat. If it wasn't so deep that you can feel it in your chest, you'd think it might be a frog.

Kupalué points at something in the water. It looks like a cluster of three eyes.

Turn to page 55 . . .

You set off on a long slog through a swampy part of the island that runs between the River Soshenstar and the River Tiryki.

At one point three zombies crawl out of the muck and begin following you. You bravely turn to face them, raising your blessed war hammer as a symbol of your faith in Clangeddin.

"Back, you foul creatures!" you shout. "Return to the graves where you belong!"

The zombies cringe at your display, then turn tail and slowly flee back through the swampland. Qawasha and Kupalué cheer your victory, and you can't help but smile as you continue toward Camp Righteous.

When you get there, though, your joy fades fast. Kupalué is the first to realize that something is wrong and signals for you to be quiet. You creep forward and discover that the templars are no longer in charge of Camp Righteous. In fact, the place is entirely empty!

"What happened?" you whisper. "I thought you said this place was safe."

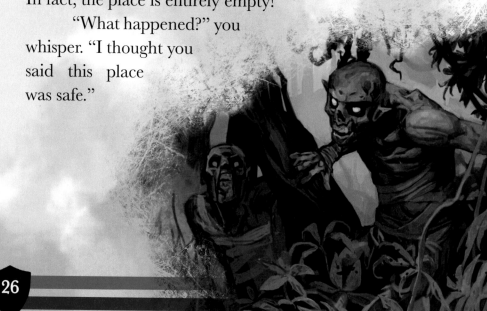

Kupalué tugs at your sleeve and makes a number of signs you can't understand. You turn to Qawasha for a translation.

"He says he thought he saw a templar uniform on one of those zombies you scared away. It was hard to tell through all the mud on them."

The druid grimaces at this news.

"I told the templars they needed to build their defenses around this place, maybe throw up a fence at least, but they just ignored me. Looks like they paid the price for that. I don't suppose it matters if the zombies got them or the goblins. They're all gone now."

Turn to page 22 . . .

With Qawasha and Kupalué in the lead, you work your way along the eastern bank of the River Tiryki toward Kir Sabal. Over the course of the days that it takes you to carve your way through the jungle there, you come to respect your guides. They may not be able to bring you directly to Artus Cimber, but they're willing to give your quest their all.

One day, as dusk is falling over the jungle, you come upon a clearing that allows you to see through the thick canopy overhead. As you gaze up into the darkening sky, you spy a three-hundred-foot-tall tower of rock in the distance. While it seems to have been naturally formed, its narrow faces fall away almost straight down from its peak. These are punctuated by several small caves, and someone has added fragile-looking ladders that run between a number of them.

A smoky fire blazes atop the tower, and you realize that it must be visible for many miles around, especially in the dark of night.

"What is that?" you ask.

"It's known as Firefinger," Qawasha says. "Word is that such signal towers once dotted the land of Chult, making it easy for the people who guarded it to communicate with one another over long distances. Most of the towers were knocked over or crumbled away long ago. As far as I know, this is the only one left."

"Then who keeps that fire lit?"

Qawasha frowns. "That's the work of a tribe of pterafolk—flying dinosaur people—who have taken over

Firefinger. They've become a plague upon this land. They like to swoop down and grab their victims, carrying them high into the sky, and then drop them to their doom."

You shudder at the thought, and as you peer at the tower, a horrible cry echoes over the land. What could you possibly have done to upset your god so much that he keeps throwing these dangers into your quest? Does he not realize that you are trying to do some good in this world?

You stare at your guides in horror as the cry grows louder.

Turn to page 21...

Y ou thank Clangeddin that you found guides sharp
enough to help you navigate such a twisty maze, or you
might have been stuck inside it forever. When you finally
reach its exit, you see that the maze wall surrounds a small
lake lined with reed huts. There's an island in the middle of
the lake, on which sits a sixty-foot-tall shrine of a giant frog.
It seems as though you could enter the shrine via a stairway
that leads into the frog's massive belly.

As soon as you step into the village, several frog-like
humanoids with brightly colored skin and gigantic eyes
approach you. They are short and gangly, with long limbs
and sticky fingers, and their skin glistens in the tropical sun.
Shortbows are strung across their backs, and they carry sharp
knives in their hands that drip with some noxious poison.

"Greetings, strangers!" a regal gold-skinned grung
shouts as he emerges from the shrine. "Have you come here
to drive away the undead who plague our land?"

Refuse to help. Turn to page 50...
Lend a hand. Turn to page 54...

E ast!" you order Qawasha.

It might have been more glorious to do battle with the pterafolk, but you're here on a mission.

You evade the flying creatures by keeping beneath the jungle's canopy, and you spend a long couple of days snaking your way through the trees.

Eventually you come to a massive gorge, through which flows a deep river that Qawasha identifies as the Olung.

"We are heading in the right direction," he advises, "although we have come out at the wrong place. The Ataaz Muhahah is nearly impassable."

Kupalué spies a high stone bridge a short way down the edge of the gorge, and you decide to cross it, even though the other end is lost in a steamy mist. You pass a large statue in the middle, and it's not until you're well past it that you realize the bridge comes to an abrupt end before it reaches the other side of the gorge.

Turn to page 34 . . .

I was not sent to Chult to hide beneath the trees," you tell Qawasha as you ready your war hammer for the coming battle. "With Clangeddin's help, we shall acquit ourselves well, and victory shall be ours!"

"Have it your way," Qawasha says as he positions himself behind you. You notice that Kupalué does the same. "Just be sure to take them down fast. Otherwise, it's up and away for us for sure."

The pterafolk circle overhead for a moment after they reach you, and then they dive straight down for you, unleashing bloodcurdling screeches as they go. You take aim at the apparent leader of the flock. As he swoops to snatch at you, you swing your hammer at his skull, knocking him out of the air.

You shout in triumph. As you turn to find your next foe, though, a pair of the creatures attack you at once, sweeping in to grab both of your arms.

You wail in fear and frustration as they haul you high into the air. You use your last breath to scream out a prayer to Clangeddin as they drop you to your death.

THE END

Frustrated, you turn back and see that the statue you passed—a Chultan warrior wearing a war mask—has sprung to life! To make matters even worse, attracted by the creature's movement, a dozen monkeys have appeared out of the misty jungle, climbing up from beneath the bridge to hoot and holler at the impending fight.

"We've apparently angered this creature," Qawasha says as he and Kupalué edge away from the stone monster.

"Should we stand our ground here?" you ask as you look around for other ways off the bridge. "Do we have any choice?"

"There's always a choice," Qawasha says. "And as the leader of our expedition, it's yours to make!"

The creature pounds the surface of the bridge with heavy fists, sending up chips of shattered stone. The river rushes by far below you. The monkeys seem to scream for your blood. You have no good choice, it seems, but you must still make one.

Fight the statue! Turn to page 38...
Look for a way to escape! Turn to page 45...

Back, foul beasts!" you cry.

Clangeddin's power flows through you as fire erupts from your hands, but it drives away only about half of the undead creatures stalking toward you. It seems he wishes you to dispatch the others in a more personal way. You wade toward the creatures, thinking you'll have Qawasha and Kupalué at your side.

Kupalué bangs his spear on the ground, and you turn to see the vegepygmy and Qawasha backing away.

"There are too many of them!" Qawasha shouts. "If it were just the undead, we might have some hope, but —"

The goblins hurl a half dozen spears in your direction. A couple of them knock down a skeleton that was about to claw at you, but another spear pierces your leg.

Your guides rush to try to help you as you fall to the ground in agony, but the zombies reach you before they do. You offer up one last prayer to Clangeddin that at least your corpse won't swell their ranks.

THE END

South!" you shout at Qawasha and Kupalué, and your guides immediately spin that way and dive into the jungle's thick underbrush.

You follow them, and not a moment too soon. From behind you come the frustrated cries of the pterafolk as they swoop into the clearing where you just stood.

"Where are we going?" you ask your guides as you hear the pterafolk skimming over the treetops above you, raking at the canopy with the tips of their wings.

"Away from them!" Qawasha answers. "After that, we'll figure it out!"

By the time night falls fully over the jungle, the pterafolk have given up their pursuit of you—at least for now. Unable to set up a proper camp for the night, you and your guides hunker down in a tight clump of bamboo. It prevents any larger predators from getting to you, although it doesn't keep away a single insect.

The next day, you hear the pterafolk overhead, and you continue to the south, avoiding any open areas that might expose you to the vicious creatures. You and your guides walk in silence so as not to alert those savage hunters.

When you finally emerge from beneath the jungle canopy, the pterafolk seem to have given up on chasing you. However, you find yourself faced with a massive wall of thorns at least twenty feet tall.

"This is Dungrunglung," Qawasha informs you. "Home of the grungs, humanoid versions of poison frogs."

"Are they friendly?"

"Much more so than the pterafolk," Qawasha says with a wide grin. "And they might have seen your Artus Cimber. To ask them, we'll have to make our way through the giant maze they've constructed out of this horrible thorny hedge."

Turn to page 30 . . .

You decide that, mission or not, you've had enough of fleeing before your foes. You're not going to give ground to this creature, whether it's made of stone or not.

"Take this, you great stony monster! If you think a dwarf is ever going to be afraid of rock, then you're dumber than what you're made out of!"

The stone golem doesn't react to your words at all. It is a creature bound by magic, not logic or emotion. It doesn't feel fear or anger, nor will it listen to your bluster. It will only work to do its job until that job is complete. Right now, that job seems to be killing you.

You utter a quick prayer to Clangeddin for both guidance and strength, then grasp your hammer with two hands and put every bit of your strength into swinging it against the golem's head. The monkeys screech around you, worked into a frenzy by the battle that is starting in front of them.

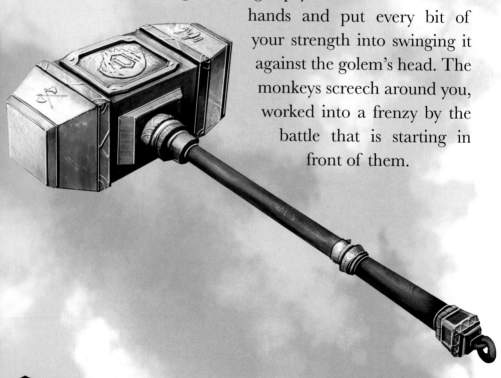

The golem moves closer and blocks your attack with its shoulder. The dense stone cracks beneath the force of your mighty blow, but it does not crumble.

"Help me!" you shout to Qawasha and Kupalué, realizing that this foe is simply too hardy to defeat on your own. "Together, we can triumph over this creature!"

Your new friends do not disappoint you. Without a moment's hesitation, Kupalué steps forward and hurls his spear at the golem. It catches the monster square in the chest, but the creature's stony skin blunts the spear's tip. The weapon goes skittering off past the edge of the bridge and tumbles away. You never hear it hit bottom.

Qawasha charges forward, his blade in hand, and slashes at the golem's head. He catches the creature on the neck, but his sword does little more than scratch it.

Undistracted by the others, the golem lowers its head and charges straight at you, knowing you are the leader of your group.

Turn to page 44...

While you hate the horrors of the undead, Clangeddin values valor in his priests, not stupidity. You might be able to take out the zombies and skeletons, but if those goblins come at you at the same time, they'll slaughter you for sure.

"Let's go," you tell your guides. "Now!"

Kupalué dashes to the northeast, and Qawasha and you chase right behind him. The zombies moan with their undead hunger and the skeletons gnash their exposed jaws. The goblins howl after you in furious protest as they watch the undead stagger after you, then follow in their wake.

Kupalué seems to know the land as if he was grown from it. He leads you through the thick jungle underbrush, and for a moment you think you're going to be able to simply run from all your problems. Then you come up against the river. You quickly search left and right, but there appears to be no bridge or other way to cross in sight.

Qawasha curses. "There's nothing for it," he says as he adjusts his pack. "We must swim!"

You consider informing him that dwarves are rotten swimmers, but you give that up when the point of a goblin's spear thuds into a nearby tree. You dive into the fast-running waters of the Soshenstar and paddle with all your might.

Your pursuers reach the shore when you're only halfway across the river. The skeletons don't pause in coming after you but the force of the river seems too much for their bones and they are quickly washed downstream. The zombies stop at the water's edge and watch the scene unfolding before them. With their prey out of reach, they turn on the goblins, and you hear the little monsters squealing in fear as they race away.

You don't have time to enjoy the pleasant sounds of the goblins' defeat, though, as you're too busy not drowning. You manage to make it to the other side of the river and collapse there for a bit until a soaking-wet and bloated Kupalué tugs you to your feet. Casting your eye about for Qawasha, you find him gasping farther along the riverbank. You allow yourselves a moment to gather your breath, then head deeper into the jungle.

Days later, you come upon another camp on the riverbank. This one, though, features fortifications all the way around it in the form of a wide ditch lined with tall sharpened stakes.

The charred corpses of people and animals surround the place, and you can see soldiers patrolling the walls and stationed in the watchtowers.

"Look!" Qawasha draws your attention to a few of the men atop the wall. "Templars from the Order of the Gauntlet! The survivors must have relocated here after Camp Righteous was overrun."

A thin but powerful-looking man with the markings of a commander waves you to the camp's front gate and meets you once you're inside.

"I'm Niles Breakbone," he says. "Welcome to Camp Vengeance."

You explain that you're looking for Artus Cimber.

"Cimber?" Breakbone exclaims. "My soldiers saw him wandering around Mbala just recently."

You want to cheer for having finally found some sign of the man, but Breakbone's scowl cuts you off. "What we really need, though, is someone to take care of my sickest soldiers. Can you help with that?"

Unfortunately, you're not advanced enough in your studies with Clangeddin to cure such ailments, and you inform Breakbone of that. His frown deepens.

"Then I insist you return your soldiers to Port Nyanzaru for treatment before we provide you with any information on where your man Cimber can be found. It really is a matter of life and death!"

Agree to help. Turn to page 25 . . .
Refuse. Turn to page 49 . . .

You realize that the gigantic stone creature isn't trying to crush you to death. It wants to push you off the bridge!

Between death by falling and death by crushing, you don't see much of a difference. It's a long drop to the bottom of the gorge, and you're determined not to go over. The golem simply weighs too much, though, and it's not about to give you a choice in the matter. It charges straight at you!

You shift your hammer to a single hand and grab at the creature with your free fingers as it comes at you. You find purchase in a crack between the rocks that make up its shoulder, and you refuse to let go.

The golem had thought it could shove you clear into the open air around the bridge, but you've thrown it off balance instead. It stumbles forward, still in your grasp, and tumbles over the bridge's edge!

As you plummet to your death, you thank Clangeddin for the opportunity to not only die in battle but do so while saving the lives of others. At least it's a fitting end.

THE END

You recognize the creature you face as a stone golem, placed here by some ancient wizard to carry out some unknown task. You're not sure what you've done to trigger it, so you don't know what you can do to placate it—other than die at its stony hands.

Refusing to give in to this fate, you start looking for another way off the bridge. There's no chance you can leap the gap at the end of it. That would just be a faster way to die, and if you're going to do that for sure, you'd prefer to go down fighting.

As you continue to search your surroundings for an opportunity, the monkeys that came out to watch the fight and are now jumping up and down, screeching in their frenzy, give you an idea.

"The vines!" you shout to Qawasha and Kupalué. "We can use them to climb down!"

Your guides dash ahead of you and start clambering down the side of the bridge and onto the last of its supports, which stab out of the greenery below. You dodge one of the golem's clumsy attacks and then sprint over to follow them, the bridge shaking beneath you as the golem continues its advance.

The footholds you find crumble instantly under your weight, and you're forced to slowly work your way down a thick, twisting vine. After a moment, though, you realize that you're not making any progress. In fact, you somehow appear to be going up instead! What is this new madness?

Craning your neck to search above for an answer to

this latest problem, you see the golem hauling your vine up onto the bridge. You desperately glance around for something else you can cling to or leap to in order to make your escape, but there's nothing within reach. If you don't do something fast, you're going to find yourself in the golem's fatal grasp, and this time you doubt there is much you can do to escape.

Clangeddin seems too busy to answer your prayers for help, and you realize that you are alone in this fight. At least Qawasha and Kupalué seem to be making progress in getting away.

Resigned to your fate, you reach for your hammer, determined to at least get a swing in at the golem before it gets its stony grip on you.

"Take that!" you cry, though you know your attack will do little to help your situation.

To your surprise, you are met not with the crushing blow that you expected from the golem but instead by massive claws

digging into your shoulders. You're torn from the vine and hauled into the air. You almost panic and try to smash your way free from your new attacker's grasp, but you realize that if you succeed, you're sure to fall to your doom. Below you, the golem watches your escape with an expressionless face, and you are at least glad to have gotten out of its warpath.

When you glance up, you see that you're in the claws of a feathered humanoid with the head of an eagle—an aarakocra, you presume—and it isn't alone. One of its friends has Qawasha, and another has Kupalué. They're hauling you higher and higher into the sky.

Demand to be set free! Turn to page 57 . . .
Ask about Artus Cimber. Turn to page 62 . . .
Go along for the ride. Turn to page 65 . . .

You inform the commander that you have more pressing matters to which you must attend. You can't let Artus Cimber get farther away.

"Fine," Breakbone says. "We'll have the three of you staked out in front of the walls to serve as zombie bait. Guards!"

Fortunately for you, Qawasha and Kupalué already have their weapons out. "Take him!" Qawasha orders the vegepygmy.

Quick as lightning, Kupalué corners the commander and puts the sharp end of his spear against the man's belly. Breakbone freezes and orders his soldiers to back up.

"Now," Qawasha says firmly, "you're going to let us go on our way or my little friend here is going to spill your last meal out onto the ground."

To your relief, moments later you find yourself outside Camp Vengeance's gates, sprinting away at top speed.

"Don't stop until we reach the trees!" Qawasha shouts over his shoulder.

Arrows zip past your head, and you can hear feet tramping behind you. You don't look back.

Turn to page 60...

W e don't have time to reinforce your excellent efforts here," you tell the gold-skinned grung. "We're looking for a man named Artus Cimber."

"You're wasting our time!" the grung leader shouts. "You either help us or you get out!"

You try to protest and explain the situation, but a score of the little grungs surge from the lake and cut you off from proceeding any farther into their village. Then they force you at knifepoint to retreat back into the thorn maze.

Unfortunately, your guides can't seem to find a way out of the place. You wander about for hours until you start hearing the all-too-familiar groans of the walking dead. The power granted you by Clangeddin helps you drive some of the zombies away as you bombard them with the fire that pours from your hands, but there are far too many. Soon they overwhelm you, and not too long after that, you and Qawasha join their ranks.

THE END

The golden grung introduces himself as King Groak, the leader of the people of Dungrunglung. "I am thrilled to have such good and powerful friends as yourselves. Tonight you feast with us!"

A wild cheer goes up among the grungs, and they escort you forward to sit on the edge of the lake with King Groak. There, when you finally have a quiet moment, you ask the grung leader about Artus Cimber.

King Groak gives you a sad shake of his head.

"I have not seen such a person as you describe. Not around our wondrous and safe home, at least. However, I will instruct my people to look for him and to report back with any news they might find. If he has wandered within a day's travel of our amazing abode, I will hear about it for sure!"

You're disappointed by this news, but you readily accept the king's offer of help.

"Now, let us talk no more of such things!" he says. "Today is a day of celebration!" He slaps his long-fingered hands together and flicks his yard-long tongue, at which a dozen blue-skinned grungs come out to take you and your guides away to prepare for the feast.

Your new friends bathe and pamper you in a way you've never experienced. Once you're clean, they paint your skin a golden hue to match that of the king himself. You're not sure how comfortable you are with such treatment, but if it helps the natives see you in a kinder light, you're not about to argue.

Qawasha is painted not gold but orange, and Kupalué remains relatively green because his moldy exterior doesn't take paint all that well, but you can see that an honest effort was made to spray him silver.

Your new friends bring you into the first floor of the shrine—a large single room—where you find King Groak waiting for you. The front part of the room is occupied by a pool of clear water lined with glowing fungi. The king sits in the back of the room, in a basin of water raised ten feet off the floor, and at his signal, the feast begins.

"I had this shrine built as a tribute to my beloved goddess, Nangnang," says King Groak. "Do you think she could possibly be anything but impressed by my efforts?"

You agree that no one could resist such flattery, but when the king presses you for more details, you devour your food instead and decline to answer him with a full mouth. You hadn't realized how hungry your time in the jungle had made you, and you stuff yourself silly.

Unfortunately, that night, you learn that food that's good for grungs isn't always good for dwarves — especially when it's eaten raw. You die clutching your belly and praying to Clangeddin for relief.

THE END

Of course we will help you!" you tell the golden grung. "Any souls stalwart enough to stand against the evils of the undead are friends of Clangeddin and his faithful!"

"Then prove your faith!" the golden grung shouts. At a gesture from him, a secret door in the thorn maze swings wide, and a handful of zombies that had been trapped inside surge out.

The grung warriors use spears to herd the undead monsters toward you. As they get closer, you step in front of Qawasha and Kupalué and hold your blessed hammer high before you.

"Get back, foul creatures!" you shout at the zombies. "By the power of the great god Clangeddin, I banish you from these people's home!"

The zombies cower before you and rush back into the maze. The grungs send up a cheer, and the golden grung favors you with a wide smile as he swims elegantly from his island to the lake shore.

Turn to page 51 . . .

F roghemoth!" Qawasha shouts. "Flee!"

You look about, unsure of what your guide means for you to do. You're on a boat with nowhere to run to. Then he and Kupalué dive straight into the murky waters of the Soshenstar.

The sick soldiers cry out for help, and you stay with them and begin uttering prayers to Clangeddin. When the creature attached to those eyes leaps out of the water, though, you realize that no amount of prayer will save you from your fate.

It is the size of an elephant, and it moves on a giant pair of frog-like haunches. It has a pair of tentacles in place of each arm, and it whips them at the boat while still in the air, ensuring you can't escape. It arcs down at you out of the sky, and the last thing you see is its gullet coming straight for you.

THE END

L et me go!" you demand as you ready your hammer for an attack against the aarakocra that has you in its clutches. You've had enough of jungles for today, but at the moment, being hauled into the sky seems far, far worse.

You're a dwarf. You prefer to be underground, deep beneath the mountains where it's cozy and safe. You've already had to take a boat to get here, across the sea! And now you're flying wildly through the air with nothing beneath you at all—and you're sick of it!

"Put me down!" You take a swing at the aarakocra, which somehow manages to angle itself out of the way. It squawks at you in a language you can't understand.

You're not about to let this monster tear you apart. What dwarf would remain calm and collected in the face of such horrible treatment?

You feel like you can't breathe! You just want to be back on solid, unmoving, beloved ground. The firmer the better!

You take another swing at the creature, and this time it can't avoid your well-aimed blow. It opens its claws and lets you go.

For a stomach-dropping moment, you free-fall through the open air, losing your hammer and windmilling your limbs all around. That doesn't seem to keep you in the air for even an instant longer.

You land hard, but you haven't fallen as far as you feared. Still, your right leg gives way underneath you with an audible and painful snap, and you collapse back onto what you realize is the exact same bridge from which you'd been trying to escape.

Perhaps you should be grateful that your supposed rescuer didn't drop you directly into the open gorge. That fall would have killed you for sure. Unless a treetop had broken your fall. Or you'd fallen into the river. Either of which would have probably killed you too, you realize.

Still, you find it hard to feel any gratitude knowing you are back where you started.

You try to struggle to your feet, but your right leg isn't about to cooperate. Instead, you hop up onto your left and see the stone golem standing there, waiting for you.

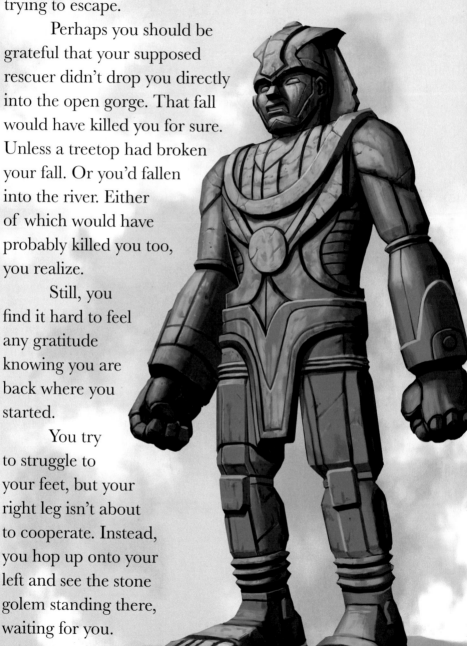

Maybe you should have played dead. That might have convinced the golem to leave you alone. Or maybe the creature would have simply pitched you over the side of the bridge to make sure you were gone.

But it's too late for that now. You stare up at the golem and beckon to it with your empty hands.

"Well?" you ask. "What are you waiting for? If you want me dead, you're going to have to earn it!"

You say a short and sweet prayer to Clangeddin, thanking him for the chance to at least die in battle rather than from a fall. Then you wait for the golem to come at you.

When it does, you roar with delight and set to pummeling it with your bare hands, ignoring the pain that it brings, right up to the very end.

THE END

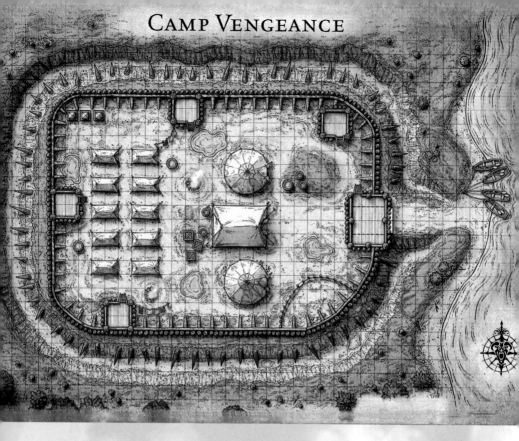

You make it to the trees, but even there, under their cool shade, you're not yet safe. You can hear Commander Breakbone still screaming from the wall around Camp Vengeance.

"Stop those traitors! They'll bring zombies back to kill us all in the night! We can't afford to let them survive!"

"Just keep running," Qawasha shouts. "Don't stop!"

He seems to be handling the run well, but you're already almost out of breath. You put everything you have into your escape, though, remembering that you don't need to run forever. Just longer than the soldiers on your tail.

At one point, you emerge into a clearing, and you can

see a ruin looming on a high plateau. You don't know what might live there, but it probably can't be as hostile as the people from Camp Vengeance.

You motion toward it, and Qawasha sees it and smiles.

"That's Mbala! The place where they said they saw your friend Cimber!"

Hope leaps in your heart. You're so close to finding the man you've come all this way for. You just need to escape your pursuers.

A spear flies past your shoulder, and you give thanks to Clangeddin that it missed you. He must have a nasty sense of humor, though, because the next spear the templars of Camp Vengeance throw catches you right along your shoulder.

It burns like fire and leaves you bleeding, but you count yourself lucky that the spear didn't score a solid hit. Otherwise, you'd be lying on the ground, maybe already dead. As it is, you still have a fighting chance.

Qawasha slows down enough to grab you by the elbow.

"We might be able to lose them in the marsh," he suggests.

Head for Mbala. Turn to page 69...
Dive into the marsh instead. Turn to page 71...

W ait a minute!" you order the aarakocra holding you in its talons. The creature snickers at you as you grab at its legs in panic. "Where are you taking us?"

"Back to our eyrie," she says.

"I don't want to go to your eyrie," you tell her.

"All right," the aarakocra says with another snicker. "Whatever you say. Where do you want to go?"

You realize that you don't know.

"I'm looking for a man named Artus Cimber. Have you seen him?"

"Personally, no. But I heard that others did. Off to the southwest. I can take you in that direction."

"That'll do," you tell her, and she changes course to fit your will.

The other aarakocra follow her, flying in formation. Qawasha shouts at you, trying to talk you into going to the eyrie instead, but after his voice becomes hoarse, he gives up.

After a while of flying inelegantly through the clouds you spot a frost giant lumbering below, an enormous creature who must be a long way from home. Frost giants usually live in the northern parts of the world—often atop snow-capped mountains. You wonder why such a massive being would be here, and how he managed the journey. What size boat would it take to carry him across the sea?

As you're gaping down at this frost giant, a gigantic boulder whizzes past you from the hand of another, who has been lying in wait beneath the canopy. The aarakocra carrying you screeches in surprise and flinches at how close the rock came to her. This causes her to lose her grip on you—and you to lose yours on her.

Stunned, you tumble into the open sky.

Turn to page 68 . . .

"T"hank you!" you say to the aarakocra. "You saved my life!"

"My pleasure," the eagle-person replies. "We're happy to help people out when we can. It's just lucky that we were flying by when that stone golem came to life. We're often too late to save the unfortunate souls that creature attacks. But shiny things like you often attract my people."

You thank Clangeddin that you keep your armor polished enough to gain such attention.

"Where are you taking us?" you ask, hoping that you might find your feet back on the ground fast.

"We live in an eyrie called Kir Sabal."

"Just like I told you!" Qawasha calls from where he's hanging from the talons of a nearby aarakocra. "They're the people we were going to see to ask about your missing friend!"

You cling to the aarakocra above you, appreciative of what she's done for you but still terrified that she might drop you at any moment. As light as she is, she must be fragile, but her wings are clearly strong enough to keep you both aloft. Despite how heavy a burden you must be for her, she carries you safe and sound until you arrive at Kir Sabal.

Kir Sabal turns out to be an ancient monastery set on a high plateau, reclaimed by the eagle-people for their own purposes. The lowest of the several connected buildings stands at least five hundred feet above the jungle floor, giving you a commanding, if dizzying, view of the lands surrounding it. It seems as if dozens of aarakocra are landing and taking off

constantly from this place, and you feel as if — despite how high it is — you've finally found a decent form of civilization in the heart of this jungle-clad land.

The creature carrying you brings you to the largest of the buildings in the monastery and deposits you on the wide balcony there. As you, Qawasha, and Kupalué goggle at the tremendous height at which you are currently standing above the jungle floor, an elderly aarakocra wings down to join you. "This is Yingmatona," your rescuer explains. "Our Teacher."

"Welcome to our home, revered guests," the white-feathered aarakocra greets you. "You can stay with us for as long as you treat us like family."

"Thank you for your hospitality," you say to Yingmatona. Unnerved by your surroundings, you decide to cut straight to the matter at hand. "I'm here looking for a man named Artus Cimber. Would you happen to know where he is?"

Yingmatona arches her neck and lets out a loud screech. A pair of younger aarakocra wing down from above and land next to her. She says something to them in their chirpy language, and then the pair leap from the platform and soar off to the southwest.

"Artus was here recently," Yingmatona explains. "I've sent my two fastest flyers out to see if they can track him down."

You thank her for her kindness, and she acknowledges your comment with a wave of her wings. She arranges for quarters for you and your guides, and then she leaves you to wait.

The next morning, just before noon, the flyers return. One of them has a man in his claws, whom he sets down on the balcony. The man smiles at you.

"Hello," he says. "Sorry to be late. We had a terrible time evading the pterafolk. I hear you're with the Harpers. I'm Artus Cimber."

Ask him about the ring. Turn to page 75 . . .
Ask him why he left the Harpers. Turn to page 77 . . .

You scream the whole way down, and the aarakocra screech like a choir of demons as you go. You send up a final prayer to Clangeddin and wonder in your heart why you had to die like this rather than with a foe in your grasp.

To your surprise and immense relief, you land not crushed on a rocky plain or impaled upon a tree as you'd feared you would, but instead in the relatively warm, safe, and massive hands of a frost giant. As you lie there stunned, the giant gazes down at you with an eye as large as a melon and begins to laugh with a low rumble that sounds like thunder.

"What presents does the sky offer us in this strange, hot land?" the giant says.

"Who are you, little one?" the other giant says as he peers down at you, just as curious as the first.

You've never met a giant before, and you open your mouth with no idea what you should tell them.

Lie. Turn to page 78...
Tell the truth. Turn to page 84...

You don't like the smell of that swamp. You shake your head at Qawasha.

"Dwarves don't swim well. We prefer the mountains."

"Mbala it is!" Qawasha says. "There's only one thing we need to do to make that happen."

"What's that?"

"Run faster!"

Despite the horrible wound in your shoulder, you dig down to find reserves of energy you didn't know you had left. You reach the edge of the plateau you saw before, and without another word you start to climb.

This at least is something you know how to do, as much as it hurts. You're a dwarf, and the cliff you're climbing is made of rock. You can find the faults in it, the paths on which you can crawl. This makes so much more sense to you than the overgrowth of the jungle you left behind.

As you grit your teeth and climb higher, you hear the clatter of a spear hitting the wall below you. You're already out of reach of the tired soldiers chasing you. One of them leaps up to climb after you, but you start knocking loose rocks down on him from above, and he quickly gives up on that idea.

Kupalué finds a path that cuts across the cliff face, and you collapse upon it. After a while, you recover enough strength to start walking once more, until you reach the top of the plateau. The path is littered with human skulls, but you push past them, too close to give up now.

There may have been a city up here once, but now

there's only an old ruin and a single hut still standing. As you approach the hut, an old woman emerges and introduces herself.

"I am Nanny Pu'pu."

Your wound finally overwhelms you, and you collapse in front of her.

"You're dying," she tells you softly. "But I can bring you back from the dead to a half-life at least. All I need from you is the soul of another."

Ask if there's another way! Turn to page 82 . . .

Refuse to trade another's life for yours. Turn to page 86 . . .

You won't be any good for finding Artus Cimber if you're dead.

"The marsh it is!" you shout at Qawasha. He and Kupalué charge straight for it, with you tramping hot on their heels.

The marsh is filled with long tracts of mud and wide, shallow stretches of water. To a dwarf who prefers the dry comfort of tunnels carved deep under a mountain, this is possibly the worst part of the jungle yet. How can you trust even the ground if it has become like a trap beneath your feet?

With the help of your guides, you manage to avoid getting stuck in the mud, although many of your pursuers are not so fortunate. They wind up trapped waist-deep in muck, shouting for their fellows to help them.

A handful of the soldiers don't give up chasing you, though, and the going is painfully slow. Every now and then an arrow comes worryingly close, and you are concerned that you are not managing to put enough distance between you and your pursuers. Just when you are beginning to think this is all rather hopeless, Kupalué points toward a watery part of the marshes and signals to Qawasha in a way you can't quite understand.

"We need to dive into the water!" Qawasha translates in a harsh whisper.

You're not sure of the wisdom of this, but once Kupalué slips beneath the marsh's surface, you don't have much choice but to follow.

The water is warm and filthy, and you can't see past your hands in it, but you dive as deep as you can and stay down until the burning in your lungs demands that you surface. Unfortunately, you lose track of your guides in the murky water. Due to the presence of the soldiers, you can't call out for them, and they can't do the same for you.

You dive back into the water, over and over, evading the soldiers and praying to Clangeddin to help you find your guides. Hours later you realize you're hopelessly lost. Finding a dry patch of land, you wait there until nightfall. The soldiers light torches to help them find their way through the marsh, which in turn helps you keep track of them. Soon they move off, complaining loudly about how they can't see well enough to find you in the darkness, and you allow yourself to relax slightly.

Late that night, when the last of the soldiers have disappeared, you risk calling out for Qawasha and Kupalué, but they never answer. No one does, and you wonder if even Clangeddin himself has abandoned you. But you resolve to keep the faith.

When morning comes, you look for some sort of landmark to guide you out of the marsh, but you don't see anything you recognize. Dark clouds hang low over the marsh, obscuring the sun, so you don't even know what direction you're facing. There are a few mountains — maybe even volcanoes — in the distance, but you don't know which ones they might be.

You pray to Clangeddin for guidance, but perhaps

you're too far from your homeland for him to be able to help with such requests. However, he does relieve some of the pain in your badly wounded shoulder, though it is not healed completely. You expect you will need further assistance from him before it is.

For days you wander around the marsh. There's plenty to drink, but your food starts to run low. You've never been much of a hunter, and you don't recognize many of the plants in this land as safe to eat. Soon you're going to have to try whatever you can get your hands on, no matter the consequences, or starve to death.

You've become a bit delirious with hunger when you finally hear voices approaching. Someone else is there with you! But are they your guides or other kind souls that might help you? Or are they the soldiers—or something even worse?

Clangeddin doesn't offer any guidance as to whether they can be trusted or whether you should keep yourself hidden from sight. You are at loss for what to do, but the decision can be made only by you.

Hide! Turn to page 90 . . .
Call for help! Turn to page 92 . . .

You introduce yourself and tell Artus, "The Harpers are concerned that you ran off to Chult with the Ring of Winter without leaving word behind. They thought you'd been kidnapped or killed."

Artus spreads his arms wide and gives you a wary smile. "As you can see, I am both alive and well."

"This ring really seems to have people worried," you muse aloud.

The man removes the ring from his hand. You can see that it is rimed in frost, even on such a sweltering day. He holds it up for you to examine.

The aaracokra who brought him here goggle at the artifact, impressed with how it shines.

"In the hands of a man like myself, it's a powerful bit of magic," Artus explains as you gaze at it. "But in the hands of a frost giant like Jarl Storvald, the king of such people, it

could be used to freeze the entire world solid. It would bring about the legendary Age of Everlasting Ice."

A horrible screech startles you at that moment, but before you can reach for your war hammer, the ring disappears in a flash of leathery wings. You peer up into the sky to see one of the pterafolk gliding away, the Ring of Winter clutched in its claws.

The aaracokra with you chase the creature down and knock it from the sky in a stunning aerial battle. To your utter despair, the thief drops the ring, and it disappears into the jungle canopy.

As the ring tumbles away and is lost, you gasp in horror, but Artus shrugs and smiles. "The thing was always more trouble than it was worth," he says. "At least now I know the frost giants will never find it."

You're not too sure the High Harpers will see this so favorably, but there is little you can do now but return to them and report on this turn of events. You just hope they don't take the bad news out on the messenger.

THE END

You introduce yourself and explain, "The High Harpers were concerned. They sent me here to see why you left them so suddenly."

Artus Cimber gives you a knowing smile. "To discover what happened to the Ring of Winter, you mean."

You start to protest, but he waves you off with a chuckle.

"I may not look it, but I'm an old man, and I know where the minds of the High Harpers lie."

Artus stares down at the frost-rimed ring on his finger for a moment and shakes his head. "I came back to Chult to find a way to reconnect with my long-lost wife, Alisanda," he says. "The ring has kept me fit and healthy all these years, but I don't need it any longer."

He gazes at you, trying to take your measure. "I only brought it with me to keep it safe," he says, "but it's proven to be nothing but a nuisance."

Turn to page 81...

I'm an adventurer!" you tell the giants, believing that you can't trust them with the truth of your task. "I came to Chult to make my fortune."

They look at the state you're in and laugh.

"And how is that going for you, little one?" the first giant asks. "Shouldn't you have a bard with you to record your epic deeds for posterity?"

"I had one!" you respond, figuring that if you're going to lie, you might as well lie big. "I lost him to those awful eagle-people who dropped me into your wonderful hands."

The giants' rumbling laugh reminds you of the sound of a landslide.

"Now we know you're lying," the first one chortles.

"And desperate," adds the other.

"I am a great warrior priest of the dwarf god Clangeddin!" you insist, though something tells you there is little you can say that will frighten them into submission.

"You're an idiot," the first giant growls. Apparently he is no longer amused by you.

Sensing that you are running out of time, you reach for your hammer, but your hand finds nothing but empty air. Realizing you must have lost it in the fall, you gulp down the dread that lodges in your throat.

"Get rid of him," the second giant says, waving his hand dismissively.

"Good idea," the first giant agrees. You scream in absolute terror as he flings you far into the distance.

You arc out over Chult and see so many things

spinning beneath you: cliffs, rivers, swamps—even a village of leopard-people. One of the last things you see flash by is a wide strip of sandy beach, and then you land in the ocean, splashing deep into the warm, salty waters.

You struggle to strip off your armor, clothes, and belongings, right down to your underwear, and then you begin the long swim back to the surface, hoping to make it before the air in your lungs runs out.

As your head breaks the surface, you breathe in huge gulps of air and give thanks to Clangeddin for letting you survive so far. As you look toward the still-distant shore and set out swimming as hard as you can, you make him one more promise. If you get back to solid land, you'll give up on your foolish quest to find Artus Cimber and heed Clangeddin's call to battle instead.

THE END

You put up your hands. "If I told you I wanted the ring, you wouldn't trust me with it."

Artus laughs. "You're a sharp dwarf, I'll give you that. Whatever I do, I cannot risk letting it fall into the hands of the frost giants."

You could try to take the ring from Artus, but that would be foolish. You could return to Baldur's Gate and report that Artus is fine, but the High Harpers might send you back here to retrieve the ring from him. Chult may be a wondrous land filled with amazing people and things, but it's an ocean away. Once you return home, you plan to stick to dry land.

You pray to Clangeddin for guidance—and it comes to you.

"Let me take the ring from you," you tell him. "I swear on my sacred war hammer that I will return it to the Harpers right away."

"I've never known a dwarf to break a vow like that." Artus rubs his chin as he considers this and then breaks into a wide smile. "An excellent solution!"

You smile as well. You've found your man and ensured the safety of the Ring of Winter—and now you can return home in triumph!

THE END

Y ou don't want to hurt anyone, especially not the faithful guides who have brought you so far. There has to be another way.

Nanny Pu'pu calls your guides to your side.

"Qawasha," she says, "could you fetch me a coconut from one of the palm trees on the edge of the plateau? The water inside it might do your friend some good."

Qawasha gazes down at you with pity. He knows the coconut water won't save you, but he's not prepared to refuse to help someone who's dying. He gives you a nod and then goes off to find you a coconut.

Kupalué makes to go with him, but Nanny Pu'pu calls him back. The vegepygmy comes to your side, and you reach for his hand. He gives it to you, and you hold it tight.

You begin to cough then, and you wonder if you might never stop. When you finally do, you're exhausted, and you know the end is coming soon.

You look to Nanny Pu'pu. "This can't be the only way."

She shrugs. "You either want the half-life I can grant you or you don't."

You offer up a prayer to Clangeddin, and the answer is clear. You can't betray a friend.

Before you can tell Nanny Pu'pu to stay her hand, though, you begin to cough again, harder than ever. You don't stop. Not until you're dead.

As you close your eyes, you think, *At least I stayed true to myself. At least my friends will live.*

You open your eyes one last time, your breath already gone, and you see Nanny Pu'pu coming at Kupalué with a knife. You try to shout out a warning, but you can't speak. It's too late!

Turn to page 89 . . .

All right," you say. You're just exhausted—too tired to lie to anyone anymore, especially a giant who just saved you from a fatal landing. "I'll tell you everything. I'm a cleric of the dwarf god Clangeddin Silverbeard, and I work with the Harpers. They sent me here to look for a lost member named Artus Cimber."

The ears of the giants prick up at the mention of Artus's name. You realize that you may have made a terrible mistake, but you've gone too far down this path to turn back now.

"What an amazing coincidence," the first giant says, giving his friend a sidelong look. "Or maybe it isn't."

"We are also here to hunt for this Cimber," the second giant explains. "We have come a long way, south from the Sea of Moving Ice to this hot and horrid land, to find him and his treasure."

84

"The Ring of Winter," you say, hating every word that comes out of your mouth.

"As you might imagine, its worth is immeasurable to our tribe. We have a full score of our people here to track this little Cimber rat down and find it."

Not surprisingly, the giant's words provide you with little reassurance.

You grimace, fearing that the giants might not believe what you have to say next.

"I wish that I could help you. I have been searching for him high and low since I came to this accursed land, but I have yet to set eyes on him."

The giants frown at each other. "We believe you," the first one says after a moment. "But we need to bring you to our captain to report this."

You consider trying to run, but looking up at both the giants, you recognize exactly how futile this would be. Instead, you agree to go with them and hope for the best.

Turn to page 93...

N ever!" you tell the old woman. "What is my life worth if it comes at the cost of an innocent's, much less that of a friend?"

You realize then that you've become friends with Qawasha and Kupalué over the many days of your journey here, to this spot where it seems you will die. You feel your shoulder where the spear got you, and you realize that you've been bleeding badly from your wound this entire time. The realization makes you shiver—or is that the chill that's entered your body as your hot blood left it?

"Leave the man alone, you hag," Qawasha cries. "You think we don't know that the pile of skulls at the entrance to this place is your handiwork? We should cut you down where you stand."

Kupalué snorts an agreement and brandishes his spear at the old woman. He stands between you and her, ready to protect you with his life.

Nanny Pu'pu cackles at your guides. "If you think you can take me, you're welcome to try."

You reach out and grab Qawasha's arm. He looks down at you so sadly, you know without a doubt that you're dying.

"Just promise me one thing," you tell him. "Don't let that woman have my body when I'm gone."

He shakes his head. "We will burn your body and turn it into wisps of smoke on the wind."

"Thank you," you say. Then you begin your final prayers to Clangeddin. Your god's name is the last thing that passes from your lips, and you know that he will meet you in the afterlife.

THE END

You awaken a short time later, and everything seems so cold. It takes you a while to realize that the weather's exactly the same. It's your flesh that has lost all its heat.

You pinch yourself and feel no pain. You feel nothing bad at all—but nothing good either.

You gaze up at Nanny Pu'pu and Qawasha. She smiles at you proudly, happy to have brought you back to this hollow half-life. Qawasha glowers at you with murder in his eyes, eager to have his revenge on you for the death of his friend.

You open your mouth to speak but realize you have no air in your lungs. You stand up and draw in a purposeful breath.

"I didn't want this. I tried to stop her!"

"So you say." Qawasha gives Nanny Pu'pu a sidelong glare that she pointedly ignores. "All I know is that a traitor like you is worth far less than a vegepygmy who had such a bright soul."

Qawasha's words hurt, but you sense that the man is not willing to take up the argument with the powerful Nanny Pu'pu, who is the real culprit here. And you can't blame him, considering her obvious power.

Ask Nanny Pu'pu to bring Kupalué back to life. Turn to page 94 . . .
Ask about Artus Cimber. Turn to page 98 . . .
Threaten Nanny Pu'pu. Turn to page 108 . . .

As bad as Chult has been for you, you decide you can't afford to place your trust in luck. You hide deep in the reeds as the voices continue to approach. Eventually, you see a shallow-bottomed boat grow near, so close you have to fight the urge to shout to the occupants. But then you notice they're all wearing crimson robes and speaking with an accent that marks them as hailing from the Unapproachable East.

They can only be members of the evil cabal known as the Red Wizards of Thay.

You hunker down as low as you can manage until they pass by. Once they're gone, you wonder if you might have hallucinated the entire thing.

An hour later, a trio of creatures emerge from the marsh like great armored monsters. They're aldani, lobster-people who walk on two feet, and you can't help but scream at the sight of them.

Unsurprised by your reaction, they shush you. "Quiet, soft and fleshy one," one of them burbles. "You will bring the evil wizards down on our heads!"

"Kill me if you must!" you tell them. "I offer my soul up to Clangeddin!"

Another one of them chortles at you. "Are you so eager to die? We just want you to depart from our home and leave us in peace."

You give the aldani a bitter laugh. "I'd be happy to leave here forever."

"If you swear to that, then you have a deal."

For a moment, you think of your quest to find Artus Cimber . . . and you decide that someone else will have to finish that job. The aldani escort you back to Port Nyanzaru, and you book passage to Baldur's Gate. Before you leave Chult, though, you have a massive shellfish dinner and regret not one bite.

THE END

Y ou decide that nothing could be worse than dying here in the marsh alone. As the voices grow nearer, you stand up and start waving, hailing whoever's coming your way in that shallow boat.

As they get closer, you recognize them by their crimson robes. They're **Red Wizards** from the distant land of Thay, which they rule with an iron fist. As they spot you, every one of their faces breaks into a wicked smile, and you realize you've made a terrible mistake.

"A desperate soul?" one of them shouts with glee. "Let's have a little fun with this one!"

"Fireball or lightning bolt?" another calls out to you.

"What?" you say, confused.

"How do you want to die?" the wizard asks. "Fireball or lightning bolt?"

You open your mouth to reply, but no words come out. You cast about for a means of escape, but you're just too tired to run.

"Hey," a third wizard says. "How about both?"

THE END

The two frost giants take you to the shore, which they manage much faster than you ever could have. There they hail their compatriots and bring you aboard their ship, the *Hvalspyd,* a gigantic longship that stretches at least two hundred fifty feet from stem to stern. With the giants aboard, though, it hardly seems big enough.

They present you to their captain, a weathered female giant by the name of Drufi, and she is delighted to meet you.

"You will accept our hospitality while we are here in Chult," she says, a large smile lighting her face.

"How long will you be here?" you ask nervously.

She carries you over to a gigantic birdcage hanging near the rudder, and she slips you inside it. "Until we find this Artus Cimber and his ring."

This is not the end you envisioned for yourself, but sometimes the gods don't give you what you want, no matter how hard you pray.

THE END

You didn't mean for Kupalué to die and wish you could do something—anything—to change that. You'd swap your life for the vegepygmy's if you could, but you know it doesn't work like that.

But maybe you should ask?

"Nanny Pu'pu!" you implore. "How could you do this? Please, I beg you, bring Kupalué back to life!"

"I might be able to do that," she says as she thoughtfully strokes her chin. "But I'd need another soul for it. And I only see one other that's free at the moment." She gives Qawasha a meaningful look.

"No!" you shout as Qawasha backs away, putting his hand on the hilt of his sword. He's worried that you're going to attack him too, and after what's just happened, you can hardly blame him.

"If you so much as lay a hand on me, I will not be responsible for my actions," he snarls with barely constrained fury. "Isn't it bad enough that you murdered my best friend?"

You're not sure which of you he is addressing, but as he glances darkly at Nanny Pu'pu, you realize that if he wasn't so wary of her, the man would have already put his blade through your chest. You wonder, in the state you're in, if that would actually do you any harm.

Either way, Qawasha is obviously spoiling for a fight, and this is not the place for it. If a battle between the two of you breaks out here, Nanny Pu'pu might kill you both on the spot. Instead, you decide you want to put as much distance between you and Nanny Pu'pu as possible. You gesture toward the door, and your guide leads the way out, not taking his eyes from either of you for a moment. You leave with Nanny Pu'pu's cackle echoing in your ears.

As you hike back down toward the jungle, you try to reason with Qawasha.

"I realize you are angry with me," you say. "Can we at least have a truce about this until we reach the ground?"

Qawasha grudgingly agrees. "If I didn't finish you in front of Nanny Pu'pu the moment I realized she had killed Kupalué for you, I suppose I can wait until we are on solid ground before I shove my blade through your belly."

You wish that there were something you could say to make him understand, and you walk for a long while in silence, trying to find the words. As you near the ground, sensing that the time for all of this to come to a head is near, you try again to reason with him

"I did not want this," you start. "I would have stopped it if I could."

"You could have accepted your death like a true warrior," Qawasha snarls. "Isn't that what your dwarf god would have wanted you to do?"

That stings more than you care to admit, and you feel yourself getting angry at his stubborn refusal to listen to you.

"That's not fair," you say. "I have a mission to complete. Once that's over, I can leave this world on my own terms rather than having failed because my guides steered me into the path of a guard's thrown spear."

"You cannot blame your injury on us." Qawasha

speaks in such a dark tone that you wonder if he's going to attack you right then, despite your agreement to wait until you reach the jungle. "Perhaps if you'd been a better warrior, your god wouldn't have let you get hurt."

You realize that there is no way for you two to settle your differences that doesn't involve a fight. But after what happened to Kupalué, do you really want to win it?

You should have said no to Nanny Pu'pu immediately. Instead, your hesitation cost Kupalué his life, and you will have to live with the guilt for the rest of your half-life. You should be dead already. Is it right to fight to defend a life already lost?

Confront Qawasha. Turn to page 100 . . .
Continue down the cliff. Turn to page 105 . . .

W e are looking for a man named Artus Cimber," you tell Nanny Pu'pu. Your quest seems irrelevant now that you're at least half dead, but you realize it's all you have left. "We heard he was here."

She gives you a sympathetic nod. "He visited me earlier in the week. I believe he was heading for Orolunga."

You look to Qawasha.

He frowns at you. "I know of this place," he says. "It's an ancient city that was consumed by the jungle long ago."

"It lies to the west of here," Nanny Pu'pu says. "That's what I told this friend of yours. I can't say if he followed my directions."

"Thank you for your help," you tell her, although you're not sure that you mean it.

You lead Qawasha to the exit, considering your next steps. He glares at you the entire way.

"Look," you finally say to him, "I understand that you're angry about this, and you have every right to be. But we're stuck here in the jungle together for now. Can we put our differences aside for the moment?"

"Differences? My best friend is dead, and the blame lies at your feet."

You give him a solemn nod. "We can argue about this now and maybe kill each other. And no matter who wins, my mission will be a failure, and the Ring of Winter will be lost. Perhaps to the detriment of the entire world. Or, if you can hold your temper just a little while longer, we can recover the ring . . . and then hash this out."

Qawasha glowers at you until you wonder if he's going to attack you right then and there.

You spread your hands wide. "I don't think Kupalué needs to have died in vain."

That hits the guide hard. "I will do this with you," he says. "For the memory of my friend. And then I will kill you, for all that you have done."

"Fair enough," you say, as agreeably as you can manage. "I don't think I could ask for more. For Kupalué."

Qawasha starts down the narrow path from Mbala. "For Kupalué."

Turn to page 102 . . .

Too many people have died today already—including you.

"Look," you say to Qawasha. "If I could trade my life for Kupalué's, I would do so in an instant."

The guide turns to you, enraged. "You should have thought of that before you let that witch murder him for your own life!"

"I'm sorry about that. I truly am."

Qawasha stands there before you for a long moment, and you wonder if he's going to break your agreement and throw you off the cliff-side path.

"Go ahead," you tell him. "Destroy me. I deserve it."

He glares at you, then spits in your face before turning on his heel and continuing down the path at a breakneck pace, almost as if he can't wait to reach the bottom so he can kill you with honor instead.

You don't say a word to each other the entire rest of the way down. Once you reach the bottom, there's a bit of a clearing where the path ends. Qawasha goes to the far end of it and turns, his sword already in his hand.

"All right," he says. "Let's finish this."

Regretfully you grab your hammer and heft it in your hands. You suspect you could take the guide down, even as numb as your flesh feels now. After all, you are a trained warrior, while he has spent his life exploring. But you cannot bear to do it.

You toss your hammer to one side and spread your arms wide.

"I apologize once more," you say. "I cannot undo what she has done. I cannot bring your friend back to life."

"No more tricks!" the guide says. "Pick up your weapon and defend yourself!"

You shake your head. "You were right. I was wrong. I submit myself to your judgment."

He brandishes his blade at you but doesn't come any closer. "What in the name of your useless dwarf god does that mean?"

You fall to your knees. "I have failed in so many ways. I deserve nothing more than death. I ask that you give it to me. You more than anyone deserve the satisfaction of that after what has been done to your friend."

He approaches you slowly with his sword out before him and you resign yourself to your fate.

Turn to page 113 . . .

Qawasha leads you into the jungle to the west. After hacking your way through the undergrowth for a couple of days, you come upon a tall man with tawny skin, brown hair, and green eyes. His traveling companion is a saurial, a lizard-like person with a wrinkly gray hide. The man wears a ring rimed with frost, and you recognize it as the Ring of Winter.

"Artus Cimber?" you say.

The man gives you an uncertain nod. "And this is my friend Dragonbait."

You show him your silver pin in the shape of a harp, which marks you as a member of the Harpers.

"Ah!" he says. "This is about the ring, isn't it? The High Harpers want to make sure it's safe."

You confirm this with a nod. The man takes off the ring and holds it in front of you.

"All right," he says. "I'll give it to you—if you can guarantee you'll keep it out of evil hands." He still seems suspicious of you, and you realize that whether or not he actually gives you the ring rests entirely on how you respond to his offer.

Take it. Turn to page 118...
Refuse it. Turn to page 121...

You take a swing at Nanny Pu'pu, but she pivots out of the way of your attack. Despite her apparent age, she is as nimble as a dancer.

"You ungrateful wretch!" the green hag snarls at you. "You think you can take me on? I had the power to bind your departing soul to your unwelcoming flesh. I can unbind it just as easily!"

"By Clangeddin's shield!" you curse. "Does your evil have no end?"

Nanny Pu'pu smirks at you. "If you want to remain in my favor, then you must do me a new service."

"I am done with your deals, hag!" you shout.

She cackles once more. "You still have one friend left in this world. Kill him, and I'll let you go on your way. Fail me, and I'll return you to your rightful death!"

Qawasha gapes at you as he reaches for his sword.

Try to escape! Turn to page 116...
Attack the hag! Turn to page 110...

As you draw nearer to the ground, you realize that once you get there, Qawasha is going to try to kill you. Under other circumstances, you might have let him, but right now there is too much at stake. You must find Cimber and secure the ring before it falls into the wrong hands. Kupalué understood the mission. If Qawasha kills you now, doesn't that mean that Kupalué died in vain? But you're not sure your guide will see it that way.

It happens sooner than you had expected, though. When you reach a particularly narrow part of the path, Qawasha breaks his word to wait until you reach the jungle floor and charges forward to shove you off the cliff. As you tumble out into thin air, you flail about in terror. Your hammer catches on something, and the next thing you know, you've accidentally pulled Qawasha along with you.

Qawasha screams at you in terror and rage as the two of you fall dozens of feet into the thick jungle canopy below. Branches tear at you and snap under you but do little to slow your fall. You land. Hard.

Qawasha is dead as soon as he hits the ground. Because you are undead, you don't feel any pain from having landed so badly, but your legs no longer work. You manage to pull yourself along by your arms and stop at your guide's side.

"I'm sorry, my friend," you offer to his still form. "I will do what I can to make this right. I promise."

You fancy a small smile makes its way to Qawasha's lips before you close his eyes and pull yourself painlessly across the forest floor.

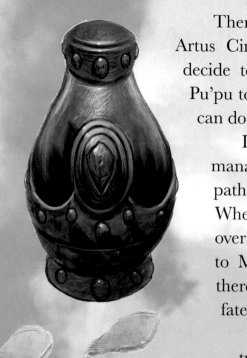

There's no chance for you to find Artus Cimber like this. Instead you decide to climb back up to Nanny Pu'pu to see if there's something she can do.

It takes you three days to manage it, pulling yourself up the path one arm's length at a time. When you finally haul yourself over the pile of skulls at the entry to Mbala, you find her waiting there for you, cackling at your fate.

"How is the afterlife treating you?" she says with open glee.

You wish that you could take her down, but you know that such an act is beyond you now.

"Poorly," you say. "I wonder if you might do me the courtesy of letting me move on?"

She gives you a disappointed cluck of her tongue. "Now, now, now. Where would be the fun in that?"

You level a devastating glare at her. You're not going to let her toy with you for another minute.

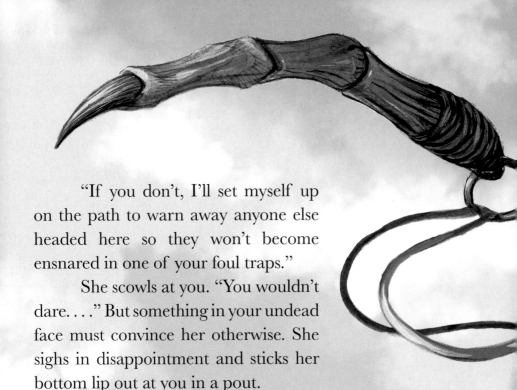

"If you don't, I'll set myself up on the path to warn away anyone else headed here so they won't become ensnared in one of your foul traps."

She scowls at you. "You wouldn't dare. . . ." But something in your undead face must convince her otherwise. She sighs in disappointment and sticks her bottom lip out at you in a pout.

"All right," she says. "I hope you enjoy meeting your precious god."

You offer up a prayer for that very thing, and she waves her hand at you and releases you from her spell.

THE END

As you turn to leave, you look down at your hands—the ones that maybe could have saved Kupalué from Nanny Pu'pu—and you begin to shudder. After a moment, you realize that you're trying to cry, but your undead body can no longer generate tears. You can't even grieve properly, whether it's for Kupalué or yourself.

You turn on Nanny Pu'pu with your full fury and stab a finger at her.

"You should have let me die!" you tell her. "Instead, you killed an innocent creature, all so you could transform me into this horrific thing!"

The woman smiles at you. "Deep down you wanted me to, my devilish dwarf. I simply made you the offer. When you didn't refuse it, you abandoned your good sense and your god's grace."

You gape at her, stunned by her vile words. "How dare you, you foul beast!"

Nanny Pu'pu begins to speak in a voice that sounds awfully like yours. "Save me, Nanny Pu'pu! Please! I'll do anything! Anything! Just don't let me die!"

As the look of horror grows on your face, she breaks into a vicious cackle that would curdle your blood if it were still pumping through your veins.

You heft your hammer in your hand. "Take care, woman," you growl threateningly, taking a step toward her.

"Or what? You'll show me your ingratitude?" She sneers at you. "If it wasn't for me, you'd be feeding the beetles in the back of my hut right now."

You glance at Qawasha, but he just folds his arms in front of his chest as he watches the two of you bicker over your deal gone bad. You'll get no help from him.

When you look back at Nanny Pu'pu, her features shift to those of a hideous green-skinned hag!

Turn to page 103 . . .

You heft your hammer before you and head toward Qawasha as if you're going to attack him. He gazes at you in horror as you approach him, but then, at the last moment, you spin about and swing at Nanny Pu'pu instead! You can almost hear his sigh of relief.

The hag screeches in dismay as she realizes that you've turned against her.

"You'll regret this," she says, "but not for long!"

Your first attack misses Nanny Pu'pu by a hair, but you swing at her again. This time, your hammer catches the hag on her shoulder, and you hear a satisfying crack. She cries out in pain and clutches at her broken arm.

"You're already dead," she says to you. "I just need to cut the strings tying you to this world."

Qawasha leaps forward then and stabs at the hag. Distracted by her fury at you, she doesn't see him coming until it's far too late. His blade slides between her ribs and then comes back out with a sickening sound. If she were human, the blow would have killed her for sure, but to your dismay she is still standing.

Unfortunately for you, she has time to undo the spell she cast, and you feel the energy that moved your limbs leach away. You collapse to the ground, your hammer thudding at your feet.

Qawasha doesn't come to your aid. Instead, he presses his attack against the green hag. Within seconds, he cuts her down, and she crumples into a pile next to you on the ground.

With Nanny Pu'pu no more, Qawasha turns his sword toward you, unsure whether you still present a threat. When he sees that you are never going to rise again, he sheathes his blade and kneels next to you, grimacing at the ruin you've made of yourself.

Turn to page 119 . . .

As Qawasha reaches you, you close your eyes and offer up a prayer for Clangeddin's forgiveness. You fully expect to feel the man's blade slice through your neck. Instead, you feel the weight of a hand on your shoulder.

"Rise," he says to you. "One killing never solves another. And putting an end to you cannot bring Kupalué back. That's vengeance, not justice."

Qawasha helps you to your feet.

"What about recompense?" you ask, though you can barely disguise your relief.

"How could anyone make up for the loss of Kupalué?" Qawasha asks.

You set your jaw. "I'll take his place—for as long as my legs can hold me."

This suggestion brings the ghost of a smile to Qawasha's face. "You would do that?"

"I insist," you tell him. "I work cheap. I don't need to eat or drink. I just need a purpose. This work would give me that."

Qawasha considers you for a while, then puts out his hand to shake yours. "Then you, sir, are hired."

THE END

With Qawasha leading the way, you begin the long hike back to Port Nyanzaru. As you go, you realize that your undead body is starting to break down. There's no way that you'll survive an ocean voyage, even if you could find a ship willing to give you passage.

"I'm so sorry about what happened to Kupalué," you tell Qawasha. "I don't expect you to forgive me, but I'm afraid I must beg one last favor from you."

Qawasha grunts in distaste and turns his face away from you. You continue nevertheless.

"Over the course of our journey through Chult you've proven to me that you have the stalwart heart of a hero."

Qawasha doesn't bother trying to disagree with you, and you fight to restrain a smile before going in for the killer question.

"Would you be interested in becoming one of the Harpers? They're not all ill-fated souls like me."

He turns back to you in surprise, perhaps not sure he has heard your offer correctly. As he studies you, his expression slowly softens, and you sense that you have come to some sort of an understanding.

"Misguided you may be," he says, "but you did whatever it took to get your job done. Although I hate you for what happened to Kupalué, I respect your dedication to your mission."

You reach into your pocket for your Harpers pin and offer it to him.

"This isn't official membership," you tell him. "But it should get you in the door."

"I've heard of the Harpers," he says as he closes his hand around the pin. "They work to do some good. The world could use more of that."

"So you'll join?"

"If they'll have me."

You breathe a sigh of relief. "Good. Because I have something else for you as well."

Qawasha gasps as you hand him the Ring of Winter. "This is an awfully big responsibility."

"For a guide, perhaps," you say. "But not for a Harper. Get it back to Baldur's Gate if you can. Or give it to the next Harper who comes looking for it. Just do your best to keep it safe."

"And what about you?" he asks.

You turn and start walking back into the jungle on your own. "Chult has all but destroyed me. It's time for it to finish the job."

THE END

You put yourself between Qawasha and Nanny Pu'pu and shout at the man, "Run!" He gapes at you for a moment before he decides to take you up on your suggestion and seize the opportunity to escape with his life.

You know that Nanny Pu'pu won't let Qawasha go that easily. In order to distract her from his run for freedom, you charge toward her. She raises her hands to greet you, her fingers curling with the gestures needed for some terrible spell. Instead of attacking her, though, you haul up short and pray that her spell has not yet had time to take shape.

"I don't want to hurt you," you cry, breaking through her mumbled spell casting.

She cackles at you. "I'd like to see you try!" But to your relief she has stopped her spell and is eyeing you curiously.

"I didn't want you to hurt Kupalué either," you continue, sure that you have her attention.

"So you say!"

"And now I'm going to prove it." Slowly you set your sacred war hammer down on the ground before her. Somewhere behind you, you hear Qawasha stumble over the skulls on the path downward and smile at the thought that at least he's gotten away.

Nanny Pu'pu stares at you, eyeing up the amulet that hangs around your neck. "What sort of trick is this? A cleric giving up his sacred weapon?"

"No trick at all. I don't want this shadow life you've given me. It's tainted with the death of an innocent."

"You can't just give it back!" She laughs, though she

still watches you intently as you step over your discarded weapon toward her.

"Why not?" you ask. "Surely it is within your power to undo what you have done?" You step closer to her, and she shudders at your question.

"Why would I want to?"

"Because I cheated you."

She looks confused for a moment, so you continue. "I didn't kill Kupalué. You killed him yourself. I didn't hold up my end of the bargain, so it's only fair you should take back yours."

She marvels at you as though you are like nothing she has ever seen before. "You really want to die?"

"I'm already dead," you point out. "I just want you to let me rest."

She rubs her chin and sizes you up. You offer a silent prayer to Clangeddin, and she answers it.

"Fair enough," she says. "The deal's off!"

You fall over dead—but smiling.

THE END

You don't know if you deserve to carry the ring, but you've come so far and sacrificed so much. You can't bear to let it slip away from you now.

"I swear to you," you say solemnly to Artus Cimber, "on my faith in Clangeddin and my vocation as his cleric, I will make sure it's well taken care of."

Artus considers your promise for a moment, and you're not sure whether you have done enough to convince him of your good intentions. Then he smiles and hands the ring over to you.

"That ring and I have been through a lot. I'll always be grateful to it for keeping me fit and healthy while I search for my long-lost wife. Still, I don't suppose I'll need it once I find my way back to her. Better that the Harpers make some use of it."

You thank the man profusely, barely able to believe that you have actually completed your quest. He congratulates you, and then he and his saurial friend disappear into the jungle again.

Turn to page 114 . . .

Using your last breath—and knowing that you will never be able to draw another—you offer up a final prayer to Clangeddin and beg Qawasha for forgiveness. "I know that I do not deserve it, but I hope that you can find it in your heart."

Qawasha watches as the final spark of life escapes from you, and he reaches down to close your eyes. In your final moments, you hear his voice as he speaks to you.

"You cost me a good friend, but you saved my life in the end. I may not be able to forgive you, but I hope that you redeemed yourself, at least in the eyes of your distant god."

You hear him stand to leave. "For my part, I promise to tell the tale of the dwarf priest who came to Chult to find someone—but who found out exactly what he was made of instead."

Then all is darkness and you hear no more.

THE END

I…" You look down at your hands as you reach for the ring and realize you can't keep that kind of promise. What right do you have to take the ring now?

"Look at me," you say. "I was so desperate to complete this quest for the Harpers—to do some good in this world—that I allowed myself to become something evil. You can't give me the ring. The moment you do, it falls into evil hands."

There's a horrible stench of brimstone, and you realize it's coming from the saurial.

"Dragonbait!" Artus says as he tries to wave the smell away. "His people communicate through strong scents. He makes that one when he's confused."

Qawasha puts a sympathetic hand on your shoulder. "Refusing the ring is the right thing for you to do. You continue to surprise me, dwarf. And this time in a good way."

"If you're sure, I'll trust your judgment," Artus says, slipping the ring back onto his finger.

"You need to keep that safe," you tell Artus. "Others are hunting for it, and if they find you, they'll take it from you. We can't risk it going to the wrong people."

"They'll try! Do me a favor, though," Artus says to you. "Get a message back to the High Harpers for me and let them know I'm alive and well—and that the Ring of Winter remains safe with me."

You shake hands with the man you traveled across an ocean to find. And whom you died—and killed—for while trying to reach.

"I don't think I'll get a ship to take me home," you tell him. "But I'll send a letter on the fastest ship I can locate."

"Then that will have to do."

With nothing left to discuss, Artus and Dragonbait take their leave of you and disappear back into the jungle. Soon, it seems as if they had never been there.

When you finally reach Port Nyanzaru once more, you write the letter to the Harpers that Artus requested. You also tell them that you're dead and won't be coming back. You hand the letter to Qawasha and ask him to deliver it.

"And what will happen to you?" he asks.

"No ship will take me home, but that's not going to stop me from trying to get there." You walk straight into the sea, which swallows you whole as you leave Chult behind for good.

THE END

The images in this book were created by Aleksi Briclot, Autumn Rain Turkel, Chris Dien, Chris Seaman, Christopher Bradley, Christopher Burdett, Conceptopolis, Daarken, David Hueso, Emi Tanji, Eric Belisle, Hector Ortiz, Julian Kok, Justin Sweet, Mark Behm, Mark Molnar, Matt Stawicki, Mike Schley, Olga Drebas, Raphael Lübke, Richard Whitters, Shawn Wood, Steve Prescott, Tyler Jacobson, Victor Maury, Wayne England, and Zoltan Boros.

The cover illustrations were created by Conceptopolis and Chris Seaman.

CANDLEWICK
ENTERTAINMENT

Copyright © 2018 by Wizards of the Coast LLC
Written by Matt Forbeck
Designed by Crazy Monkey Creative and Rosie Bellwood
Edited by Kirsty Walters
Published in the U.K. 2018 by Studio Press,
part of the Bonnier Publishing Group.
All rights reserved.

First U.S. edition 2018
Library of Congress Catalog Card Number pending
ISBN 978-1-5362-0246-5 (hardcover) 978-1-5362-0241-0 (paperback)
18 19 20 21 22 23 WKT 10 9 8 7 6 5 4 3 2 1
Printed in Shenzhen, Guangdong, China
Candlewick Press, 99 Dover Street, Somerville, Massachusetts 02144
visit us at www.candlewick.com

Don't miss the other Dungeons & Dragons® Endless Quest® titles!

Escape the Underdark
To Catch a Thief
Big Trouble

Or these Dungeons & Dragons titles available from Candlewick Press:

Monsters and Heroes of the Realms
Dungeonology